Lonissa

WALT DISNEY
PRESENTS
THE LITTLE MERMAID

Ariel Above the Sea

By Lyn Calder
Illustrated by Franc Mateu

A GOLDEN BOOK · NEW YORK
Western Publishing Company, Inc., Racine, Wisconsin 53404

Ariel is a little mermaid.
She lives under the sea.
Under the sea
there are shells.
Under the sea
there are fish.

Under the sea
there is Triton.
He is Ariel's father.
He is also King of the Sea.
There are other mermaids.
They are Ariel's sisters.

And here is Sebastian the crab.
He is going to lead the singing.
"Are you ready to sing?"
asks Sebastian.
"We are ready,"
say the mermaids.

5

The mermaids begin
to sing,
"We are the mermaids.
Here is our song.
We live under the sea.
It is where we belong."

The mermaids look for Ariel.
Her voice is like a bell.
"ARIEL!" calls King Triton.
"Where are you?"

Ariel is swimming
up, up, up.

"Wait for me!"
says Flounder.
Flounder is Ariel's friend.
He goes where Ariel goes.

Ariel and Flounder swim
up above the sea.
There are no shells.
There are no fish.
But there is sky.
There is a moon.
And there is a ship!

The ship has many people on it.
There is a prince on the ship.
His name is Prince Eric.

"Oh, I want to meet him,"
says Ariel.
A man sings.
The people dance.
Ariel watches them.

Under the sea
Sebastian is looking for Ariel.
"Have you found her yet?"
asks Triton.
"No," says Sebastian.
"Keep looking!" says Triton.

"Oh, I want to meet him,"
says Ariel.
A man sings.
The people dance.
Ariel watches them.

Under the sea
Sebastian is looking for Ariel.
"Have you found her yet?"
asks Triton.
"No," says Sebastian.
"Keep looking!" says Triton.

"Psst," says a clam
to Sebastian.
"Up. Swim up.
You will find her."

Ariel is still
above the sea.
Ariel begins to sing,

"I want to live
where people live.
I want to sing.
I want to dance.
I want to be
above the sea."

"Woof! Woof!"
It is Max.
Max is a dog.
He hears Ariel.
He smells Ariel.
He sees Ariel.

"Woof! Woof!"
"Come, Max,"
says the prince.
Ariel watches them go.
Then she and Flounder
swim away.

Bump!
She swims into Sebastian.
"Your father is
looking for you,"
says Sebastian.

"I have been above the sea,"
says Ariel.
"Your father will
not be happy,"
says Sebastian.

"You are back!
Where were you?"
says Triton.
Ariel does not answer.

"Just remember who you are.
You are a mermaid.
You belong in the sea!"
says Triton.
"Yes, Father," says Ariel.

"Where did you go?
What did you see?"
ask Ariel's sisters.
"I went above the sea.
I saw the sky.
I saw the moon.

"I saw a prince.
Oh, I do like him,"
...iel.

A... ...

sing the mermaids.

Ariel needs to be alone.
She goes to her special place.
She thinks about the prince.

Ariel falls asleep.
She dreams that she
is with the prince.
"Look," she says,
"I am a human."

Ariel and the prince talk.

They laugh.

They dance.

Then Prince Eric kisses Ariel.

Ariel wakes up.
She is still a mermaid.
She is all alone.
But do you know what?

One day Ariel's dream comes true.
She marries the prince.